NO ONE IS GOING
TO NASHVILLE

NO ONE IS GOING TO NASHVILLE

—— by Mavis Jukes ——
pictures by Lloyd Bloom

ALFRED A. KNOPF / NEW YORK

Text copyright © 1983 by Mavis Jukes.
Illustrations copyright © 1983 by Lloyd Bloom.
All rights reserved under International and Pan-American Copyright Conventions.
Published in the United States by Alfred A. Knopf, Inc., New York,
and simultaneously in Canada by Random House of Canada Limited, Toronto.
Manufactured in the United States of America
First Borzoi Sprinters Edition, 1987
3   5   7   9   10   8   6   4   2

Library of Congress Cataloging in Publication Data
Jukes, Mavis. No one is going to Nashville.
Summary: Sonia, who plans to be a veterinarian, finds an ally in her stepmother
when her father refuses to let her keep a stray dog for her own.
[1. Dogs—Fiction.   2. Stepmothers—Fiction]   I. Bloom, Lloyd, ill.   II. Title.
PZ7.J9294No   1983   [Fic]   82-18901
ISBN 0-394-85609-0   ISBN 0-394-95609-5 (lib. bdg.)
ISBN 0-394-89264-x (pbk.)

For my sister, Caroline Jukes Knueppel

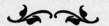

It was six o'clock in the morning.

Sonia checked her alligator lizard. He was out of termites, and possibly in a bad mood. She decided to leave him alone. Nobody else was up except Ms. Mackey, the goose. She was standing on the back deck, talking to herself.

Sonia sat in the kitchen with her knees inside her nightgown. She peered out the window. The moon was still up above the rooftops. The houses were beginning to pale.

There was a dog on the stoop! He was eating radishes on the mat.

Sonia opened the door. "Hello doggy!" she said. She knelt down. "You like radishes?"

He licked her face.

"Have you been into the garbage?"

He signaled to her with his ears.

"Stay!" said Sonia. She went back in the house and clattered in the pot cupboard.

"What time is it, Sonia?" her father called from the bedroom.

Sonia didn't answer because he had forgotten to call her "Dr. Ackley." She filled the bottom of the egg poacher with water and left it on the stoop, then went into the house and to the bedroom. "Dad," she said. "What do you think is a good name for a dog?"

He was trying to doze. "I'm closing my eyes and thinking," he lied.

Sonia waited. "You're sleeping!" she said.

He opened one eye. "Names for dogs. Let's see. Dog names. Ask Annette. She's the dog lover. What *time* is it?"

"About six fifteen," said Annette. "I heard the train go by a few minutes ago." She rolled over.

Sonia went over to her stepmother's side of the bed. "Annette!" she said. "What name do you like for a dog?"

Annette propped herself up on her elbows. Her hair fell onto the sheets in beautiful reddish loops. "A dog name? My favorite? Maxine. Absolutely. I used to have a dog named Maxine. She ate cabbages." Annette collapsed on the pillow.

"Here, Maxine!" called Sonia.

"Oh no," said her father. He slid beneath the blankets. "I can't stand it! Not a dog at six o'clock in the morning!"

The dog padded through the door and into the bedroom.

"Maxine," said Sonia, "I want you to meet my father, Richard, and my Wicked Stepmother, Annette."

Annette got up. "That's not a Maxine," she reported, "that's a Max." She put on Richard's loafers and shuffled into the kitchen.

Richard got up and put on his pants. Sonia and Max watched him search for his shoes. Max's ears were moving so wildly they could have been conducting a symphony.

"Weird ears," said Richard. He went into the kitchen.

Ms. Mackey stared through the glass at his feet and started honking. He opened the door a couple of inches. "Quiet!" he whispered. "You're not even supposed to live inside the city limits!"

She puffed her feathers.

"Beat it!" said Richard. "Go eat some snails!"

Off she waddled.

Sonia came into the kitchen wearing white pants and a white shirt with DR. S. ACKLEY, D.V.M. printed on the pocket with a felt-tip pen. She took something from the refrigerator on a paper plate and left again.

"What are we going to do about Max?" said Annette.

"Send him packing," said Richard.

"Do you really think it's going to be that easy?" said Annette.

"Yes. Sonia knows I cannot stand dogs. Neither can her mother. We've been through this before. She accepts it."

Annette turned from Richard. "Well, don't be too sure," she said.

Richard went into the living room.

"Guess what," said Sonia. "Max ate all the meatloaf." She waved the paper plate at him.

"Great, I was planning to have that for lunch," said Richard dryly. "Dr. Ackley, may I have a word with you?"

Sonia sat on the couch and dragged Max up onto her lap. Annette stood in the doorway, looking on. Sonia carefully tore two slits in the paper plate. Richard watched, his hands clasped behind his back. His thumbs were circling each other.

"About this dog—" said Richard. He walked across the room.

"You're gorgeous," said Sonia to Max. She pushed each of Max's ears through a slit in the plate. "There!" she said. "Now you have a hat!"

Max licked her. She licked him back. Richard made an unpleasant face.

"That hat looks great!" said Annette. "Where's the camera?"

Richard began again. "I know you really like the dog, but he belongs somewhere."

"With me," said Sonia. "He's been abandoned. He came to me. He passed all the other houses. He's supposed to be mine." She pulled each ear out a little farther.

Richard turned and paced. "I don't like saying no," he said. "It's harder for me to say no than it is for other fathers because we only see each other on weekends."

Annette opened the closet to look for the camera.

"But," said Richard, "since we only see each other on weekends, I have more reasons to say no than other fathers." He put his hands in his pockets and jingled some change. "Number one: I don't like dogs and they don't like me." Richard pulled out a couple of coins and tossed them in the air. He caught them. "Number two: While you're at your mother's apartment, the dog becomes my responsibility."

Annette looked at him.

"And Annette's," he added. "Anyhow, since you're at your mother's house all week long, and I would have to walk the dog—"

"I could walk him," said Annette.

"—and feed him *and* pay the vet bills—" He dropped the coins into his pocket and glanced at Annette. "I feel that it's my decision." Richard looked at Sonia. "I'm the father. And I'm saying no."

Max jumped down. He shook off the hat and tore it up.

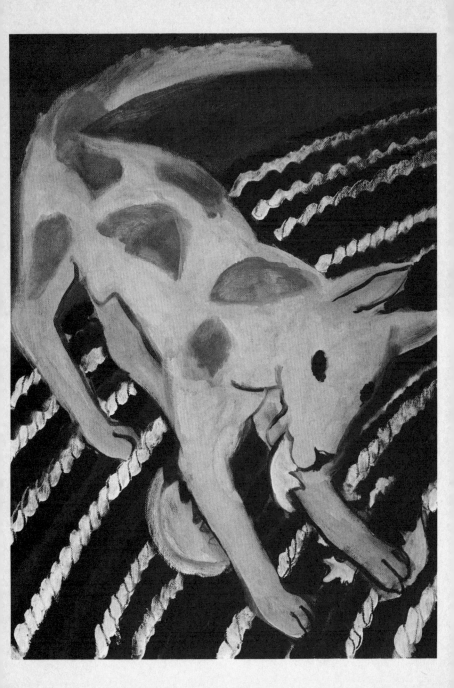

"You call me Dr. Ackley because you *know* I am planning to be a veterinarian," said Sonia, "yet you don't want me to have experience in the field by having pets."

"You're being unfair," said Richard. "I do let you have pets. Even though they abuse me. Have you forgotten this?" He displayed a small scar on the side of his finger.

"How could I forget that?" said Sonia. "Fangs bit you."

"Yes, Fangs the Killer Lizard bit me," said Richard.

"Do you remember *how* it happened?" said Sonia.

A smile crept across Annette's face. She sat down and opened the newspaper.

"I don't recall, exactly," said Richard. "And it's a painful memory. Let's not go through it."

"Well, *I* remember exactly what happened," said Sonia. "You said that you were so fast you once won a pie-eating contest, and that when you were a kid people used to call you Swifty."

Richard pretended to be bored with the story.

"And," continued Sonia, "you said you bet you could put a termite down in front of Fangs before he could snap it out of your fingers."

Richard folded his arms and looked at the ceiling.

"I said, 'I bet you can't,' " said Sonia. "Annette said, 'Don't try it.' "

Richard stared over at Annette, who was behind the newspaper trying not to laugh.

"And," said Sonia, "Fangs bit you."

"I know you're laughing, Annette," said Richard as she turned the page. "Is this my fault, too?" He pulled up his pant leg. "What do you see here?" he asked.

"A white leg with blue hairs," said Sonia.

"Wrong!" said Richard. "A bruise. Laugh it up, Annette, at my expense!"

Annette folded the newspaper. "You were teasing Ms. Mackey, and she bit you."

"Teasing Mrs. Mackey!" said Richard. "I was getting mud off my zoris!"

"Mizzzzzzzzz Mackey," said Sonia. "You were washing your feet in *her* pool, knowing she hates bare feet, and she bit you."

Richard threw up his hands. "*Her* pool. Now it's *her* pool. I built that for carp or goldfish!"

"*We* built that," said Annette.

"For whatever I wanted to put in it, and I chose a goose," said Sonia.

"No dog!" shouted Richard. He stalked into the kitchen, Annette and Sonia following him. "Send Weirdears home!" He crashed through the pot cupboard. "Where's the other half of the egg poacher?" He banged a griddle onto the stove. "No dog! Discussion closed!"

Sonia and Max went out on the stoop. They stood there a moment. Then Sonia bent down and gripped Max's nose with both hands. She looked into his eyes, frowning. "Go home!" said Sonia, knowing that he *was* home.

By the time breakfast was over and the dishes were done, Max had been sent away so many times by Richard that he moved off the stoop and into the hedge.

At noon, Richard called the pound. Sonia and Annette were listening.

Richard said, "You only keep strays five days? Then what? You must be kidding! Good-bye."

Sonia took the phone from him. She dialed her mother's number. "Hello, Mom?"

Annette left the room.

"Mom, can you and I keep a nice dog that Dad *hates* but I *love*?" Sonia glared at Richard and said to her mother, "Just a minute, someone's listening." She stepped into the closet with the telephone and closed the door. "Well, it would only be until we could locate the owner." Silence. "I *know* there are no dogs allowed in the apartment house, but nobody needs to know but us!" Silence, then mumbling. Sonia came out of the closet. "I know you were listening, Dad!"

"I admit it," said Richard. "And I'll tell you what. You really just want to locate the owner? Nobody told me that. Fair enough! You write a description of the dog. We'll run an ad in the classified section. We'll keep the dog as long as the pound would. By next weekend, we'll know something."

"Thanks, Dad!" Sonia gave him a hug.

Richard felt pleased with himself. He broke into a song.

Sonia ran to the freezer and took out four hot dogs. Then off she raced to her room for a pencil and paper. "Oops!" she said. She darted back into the kitchen and grabbed a handful of Cheerios out of the box. She opened the sliding door and threw the Cheerios onto the deck for Ms. Mackey. Then she said, "Dad? Will you please feed Fangs?"

"All right," said Richard. "I can deal with the lizard. Where's my leather glove?"

Sonia ran out the door. "Max!" she said. "Here!" She was breathless. "Here!" She fed him the hot dogs, one at a time.

Then Sonia wrote the ad:

> Found. Brown dog with a white background. Wearing paper hat. Misbehaves. Has radish breath. Answers to the name "Weirdears." Call 233-7161.

Sonia put the paper in her "DR. S. ACKLEY, D.V.M." pocket, and had a tumble with Max on the lawn. They spent the afternoon together, being pals. When it was time to go to her mother's house, Sonia hugged Max and told him: "I'll see you again, so I won't say good-bye."

Max wagged his tail in a circle.

Sonia went into the house and handed Richard the ad.

"Sonia!" said Richard.

"Dr. Ackley," said Sonia.

"This doesn't even sound like the same dog! Max isn't a 'brown dog with a white background.' He's a white dog with brown spots!"

"Same thing," said Sonia.

"Also, Max doesn't misbehave. He's very polite," said Richard.

"Then why don't you like him?" said Sonia.

Richard turned the paper over, took a pen from his shirt, and clicked it once. "Let's see."

Sonia read over his shoulder as he wrote:

> Found. White dog with brown spots. Vicinity Railroad Hill. Male. No tags. Medium-sized. Strange ears. Call 233-7161, through May 3rd.

"What does it mean, 'through May 3rd?' " she asked.

"After that," said Richard, "we're going to let someone adopt him."

Sonia fell into a swoon on the rug. "Us," she thought as she lay on the floor with her eyes shut.

"Now," said Richard. "Off we go to your mother's. We're already late."

As they were leaving, Annette picked up Max and waved his paw at Sonia. Sonia grinned.

"Ridiculous!" said Richard. He gave Annette a kiss. "Be right back!"

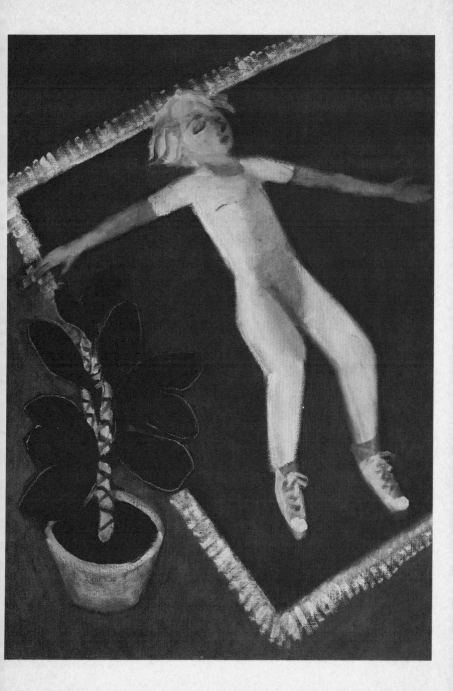

The week passed by slowly. Neither the newspaper ad nor calls to the pound and police station produced Max's owner. On Friday evening, Richard and Annette sat on the couch, waiting for Sonia to arrive. Max put his nose on Richard's knee.

Richard looked at Annette. "What does he want?" he asked.

"He's courting you," said Annette as Max licked Richard's hand.

"He's *tasting* me," said Richard. "He's thinking about sinking his teeth in my leg."

A horn beeped in the driveway. "Here she is now," Richard said. He went out on the stoop and waved.

"See you Sunday!" called Sonia's mother to Richard. She whizzed backward out of the driveway.

Sonia took the steps two at a time and ran past Richard. "Max!" she said. "I knew you'd be here!"

"Unfortunately," said Richard. "No owner."

"That's what I figured," said Sonia. "So"—she dug in her pack—"I wrote the ad"—she handed a note to Richard—"for Max to be adopted."

"Great!" said Richard. He felt relieved. "Then you *do* understand."

Neatly written, in multicolored ink, and decorated with pictures of iris and geraniums, Sonia had written:

> Free. We don't want him. A weird dog. Blotchy-colored. Has ear problems. Tears hats. Lives in hedges. Wags his tail in a circle instead of back and forth. Call 233-7161.

"Sonia!" said Richard.

She pointed to the name on her pocket.

"Dr. Ackley!" they both said at once.

"Nobody will want to adopt the dog if we say *this* in the paper."

"I know," said Sonia.

"Well, I also wrote one," said Richard. "I've already had it placed in tomorrow's paper." He opened his wallet and unfolded a piece of paper. He read it aloud:

> "Free to a good home. Beautiful, medium-sized male, Shepherd-mix. Snow white with gorgeous brown dots. A real storybook dog that will be an excellent companion. Would prefer country environment. Loves children. Sweet disposition. Obedient. Expressive ears. Call 233-7161."

Sonia looked at Richard and said, "Don't call me Dr. Ackley anymore." She turned and stormed into the kitchen. She unbuttoned her shirt and balled it up. She stuffed it into a box under the sink that was filled with bottles for the recycling center.

Very late that night, Sonia woke up. She slipped from her bed and found Max in the living room. She searched for some cowboy music on the radio. She held Max in her arms.

Annette appeared in the doorway. "What are you two doing up?"

"It might be our last night," said Sonia. "We're dancing. He weighs a ton." She turned off the radio and put Max down. "What are you doing up?"

"Restless," said Annette. "I keep hearing the trains— listen!" She put her finger to her lips. She closed her eyes. A train was drawing closer through the darkness to the station. They heard the lonesome wail of the train whistle. "It must be midnight. The freight is coming in."

Max whined softly. Sonia and Annette knelt beside him.

"I knew Mom or Dad wouldn't let me keep him," began Sonia. "Neither one of them likes dogs."

Max pushed his nose into Sonia's hand. She smoothed his whiskers. Annette said nothing.

"And," continued Sonia, "animals are better off in the country. It's just that I really believed that Max could be mine."

Annette didn't speak.

The freight train clattered away into the night. The whistle sounded faint and lost. They listened until it was gone.

Max sat with his neck stretched way back and his nose pointed up while they scratched his throat. He looked something like a stork.

"Max reminds me of Maxine," said Annette quietly.

"Really?" said Sonia. "What happened to Maxine?"

"Nobody knows for sure," said Annette. "She went off one day and didn't come back."

"Oh," said Sonia.

"We lived near the tracks—"

"Oh," said Sonia.

"My father was an engineer. One night he came home looking very sad." Annette's eyes were filling. "And my father told me—"

Sonia clutched Annette's hand. "Don't tell me. You don't have to say it."

"And my father told me that Maxine—"

Sonia hid her face in Max's neck.

"—that Maxine may have hopped a freight," said Annette, "and gone to Nashville to be a country western star."

Richard appeared in the doorway. "What's going on?" he said. "Who's going to Nashville?"

"No one!" said Annette. She stood up. "No one is going to Nashville!"

"Okay!" said Richard. "No one is going to Nashville!"

Max and Sonia got up.

Everybody went back to bed.

At nine o'clock the next morning the telephone rang. Sonia heard her father say, "Between East Railroad and Grant. About eight blocks west of the station. Come on over and see how you like him."

Richard hung up the phone. "They're coming this morning."

Sonia said nothing.

"I don't expect to be here," said Annette. "I have errands to do."

An hour later a pickup pulled into the driveway. Max barked. A woman got out of the truck and stretched. A man wearing green cowboy boots got out too, carrying a little girl wearing a felt jacket with cactuses on it and a red ballet skirt. She was holding an Eskimo Pie.

Richard walked down the steps with Max beside him. Sonia lingered in the doorway. Annette came out on the stoop, holding the box for the recycling center. Sonia's shirt was tucked between the bottles. Annette rested a corner of the box on the rail.

"Is this the dog?" said the woman. "He's a beauty!"

"Yes," said Richard.

The cowboy knelt down with his daughter. "Hey, partner!"

Max went over to them.

"Howdy boy!"

The little girl put out her hand, and Max licked it.

"Do you have a yard?" asked Richard.

"A ranch," said the cowboy. "With a lake." He patted Max. "What's your name, boy?"

"Max," said Richard.

"Why, you doggone pelican!" the cowboy told Max. "I have an uncle named Max!"

"We'll take him," said the woman. "For our little girl."

Sonia came out on the stoop. "Annette! Could you ask them about taking a goose, too?" She was blinking back tears. "And an alligator lizard?"

Annette heard a whistle. The train was coming in. "Listen!" she said. "No one is going to Nashville!" She pulled Sonia's shirt from the box. The box fell from her arms, and the bottles shattered on the cement.

"We're keeping the dog," said Annette. She almost choked on the words. She pressed the shirt into Sonia's hands.

Annette started down the steps. "We're keeping the dog!"

"Watch out for the glass!" said Richard.

Annette went to the little girl. "I'm sorry," she said. She picked up Max. She looked at Richard. "We're keeping this dog for our little girl." Tears were falling. She climbed the stairs.

"Okay! Okay! Watch out for the glass," said Richard.

Sonia was waiting. Annette put Max into her arms. "For Dr. Ackley," said Annette, "from your Wicked Stepmother and from your father, with love. Discussion closed."

MAVIS JUKES was born in Nyack, New York, and grew up in New City, New York, and Princeton, New Jersey. She graduated from the University of California at Berkeley with a B.A., taught elementary school for several years, earned her Doctor of Jurisprudence degree from Golden Gate Law School and was admitted to the California Bar. She abandoned a law career to write books. She now lives with her husband, sculptor and painter Robert Hudson, and their two little girls in Sonoma County, California.

LLOYD BLOOM was born in New York City. He graduated with honors from Hunter College, received an M.F.A. in painting from Indiana University, and has studied at the Art Students League. His work has been shown at the Society of Illustrators, and he has illustrated many books for children, including *Maid of the North, The Green Book,* and *Nadia the Willful.* Mr. Bloom now lives in Brooklyn, New York.